SNAKEBITE

By Zena Schultz

ISBN (Paperback): 978-1-9994961-2-8

ISBN (E-book): 978-1-9994961-5-9

Editing by Dustin Bilyk @ The Author's Hand
Front Cover Design by Ovila Mailhot

Printed by Ingram Spark in the United States and Canada

First printing edition 2021

Chapter One

My Antidote

I'm tired. My body needs a break. The only escape I've ever had was my star-glittered, concrete, four-walled hotel, blandly named "The Pen." So, when my last heist was smoking hot, instead of high tailing it, I looked up at the security camera and blew a kiss. Gave them a little tongue too, then I lit a Marlboro and bent my head down, broken, enjoying my last drag.

On the floor of the local trailer-town bank, on my belly I surrendered, no fighting back.

Redemption comes in different forms—a whiskey bottle, easy pussy, a loaded revolver—each short lived, each with a price. But this time when it visited me, it was different: *Fucking hope.*

After the shakes behind bars, my body finished detox. I followed the prison crowd. All the big shits went to the gym, the runts to the kitchen, but me...well, I chose the chain gang.

My hands needed a beating of a different kind. The illusion of freedom was good enough for me. At least I'd be on the other side of the barred windows. Route 66 unraveled me.

Ç

I sold my car and everything I owned—well, except for my pink laptop. Cash and a borrowed station wagon were all I needed, and the city embraced me. I followed my gut and went with it. My script made it. After winning the competition my name meant something in the industry.

But everything I've done was for him. My character. I bled for him. He bore deep into my thoughts like stitches mending a belligerent wound, only he's the one who ripped a tear in my heart. And I writhed and screamed until he came out all brand new and hungry, needing me. I guess I do have a maternal bone in my body.

I decided that going Indie was the only way for me. I wanted full control of my manuscript, an ode to the new and upcoming genre featuring "you can do it" and "never give up" kind of folks like me. After I compiled enough grants and sponsors, I took the next step, forming a group of bandits— my production team. They needed credits on a screen and I, proud mama, wanted to share with the world this life that kicked and screamed.

The only way to pacify my fucked up little man was to find him, so being the creative genius that I am, I searched the internet for the perfect casting. *Nope,* couldn't find him. The tone had to be perfect. The man had to be perfect. Despite my entire production team telling me to settle on a wannabe hipster rising star, I refused, almost ready to give up.

ς

Fuck, really? I had to get back to the city before the banks closed. Honking the horn did nothing to break through the road jam. *Why do these prisoners have to be picking up roadside garbage out here right now? Can't they just go make some license plates or something? Damn it!*

I passed by the boys in blue and white. They all looked broken, especially the lone wolf. One arm on the steering wheel, the other resting on the side of my car, as I approached him, I couldn't get over his face: his thick eyebrows, his strong chin, the gray cloud above his head. I had to shake my head and get him out of my thoughts. *But he's the one, so… forlorn.*

Shocked, I dropped everything else, including my mind, and went to call my set to tell them to quit casting because I found my lead. It was then I reached down into my attaché to find my stupid phone, and I messed up bad. Like bad.

I killed a man. Hung-over, I plowed over the lone wolf with the front end of my Subaru Outback.

Ç

"I want to get the hell out of here. Fuck," I mumbled to myself. Rubbing my eyes, I looked down to avoid the blinding sunset. Spectacular as it was, my eyes had never adjusted to sobriety or to life without Ray Bans.

'What the fuck? Is that a driverless car? Oh. That would make a cool movie,' was all I thought, then *thud*. I woke up dead. Well *almost* dead in a hospital.

After the prison made the bad move of abandoning me on the highway, they released me early on good, well, almost dead behavior.

With no medical, no family, and no money, I was banished from the emergency ward. Fucking hypocrites! What about your Hippocratic Oath? Still in prison garb, I took to the street trying to figure out where or who to go to for help. Then she came along, my black angel.

ς

"Excuse me sir?"

"You got a cigarette there, darling?" She puts her car in park, gets out and opens her passenger door. Her big brown eyes look at me with pity for fucks sake. *Bitch.*

"Sir, I'll give you a ride. Let me help you into my car." Not knowing where to go, I look disappointingly to the sky and nod my head. When I turn to look at her, well, let's just say she looks like my sister. The last time I seen her was before she passed on. I'll give this kid a chance.

"Hey. What's your name? You kind of look familiar," she asks me.

Bitch, I was a star.

She looks at me, waiting for an answer. When it's obvious I'm not saying anything, she says, "Well. Come with me. I have to make a quick stop then I can bring you home."

Chapter Two

Let It Bleed, Guisy

She did more than just knock me out. She knocked a sliver of hope into me. If I can tell anyone something important, maybe one of those mantras people love to follow, it is this: be careful what you pray for and who you pray to because it's a real kick in the ass when you get your answer. All good things come to an end and that's when the real shit starts over again.

"What's your name?" I ask the kid.

"Guisy," she mumbles back at me. I want to be rude and laugh but she seems nice enough. "My friends call me Jay." Guisy slips off her shades and throws them on the floor, "Call me whatever you want...I owe you, Sir."

"Yah, you owe me. Take me home."

"Sure, direct me," she says, smiling.

"I live on the East side. Just drive." To avoid further conversation, I roll the window down, lean back and tilt my baseball cap over my face. The corner of my slanted eye searches her over.

At first, the kid seems calm and collected, balanced, then she shocks me and grosses me out. As soon as she thinks I'm sleeping she starts chewing her nails. Like I mean going to town on her body parts. Then she does the big no-no—she picks her nose. *Gross.* But at that same stupid moment my body betrays me by releasing a little gastric bubble. Disgusted she tries to roll her window down to inhale gulps of fresh carbon city air but fails. *She deserves it.* After all, she did hit me with her car.

The drive was altogether horrible. It was disturbing, like watching a horror flick starring a baby possessed by a devil kind of bad. What she was doing to that poor clutch plate was a sin.

"Guisy, Jay, or whatever, I'll do the driving. If you continue driving the way you do the clutch plate will give out and you won't be able to switch gears. And can't you smell that burnt stink going on under the hood? That clutch is screaming for you to stop and pull over and let me drive," I say to the girl. She lights a cigarette.

"Fine," she responds.

"Thank you. Smoking will kill you, you know," I scold the kid as I search my prison pant pockets for my lighter.

As she hands me her keys, she dangles them in front of me and gets pissy. "What's your name anyway?"

I'm shocked, again. I snap the keys out of her hand and jump in the driver's side. I can't believe I'm going to drive a station wagon. More shocking though is the fact that another kid doesn't recognize me. *Ugh.*

"I used to be famous for my smile," I say.

"Is there something in your eye?"

Humph. "My name is John Clark, the Silver Fox."

Jay's fingers fly on her cell phone, "Oh. Found you. Man, you used to be a hottie!"

Really? Past tense?

"Anyway, John, I'm going to catch up on some sleep. Wake me up when we get there." She yawns and curls up to the passenger door armrest.

The drive seemed like forever, but I enjoyed the opportunity to recall my past adventures on film and television. I try not to think about the serious stuff and focus on the good, like my first call back and my first debut. It was fucking awesome, and then when I got picked up by an agent, it was even better—the party lifestyle and all the women. I had it all.

For years, I've tried to be happy and keep fit, just in case, but I've being waiting a long time and my body and wallet are feeling the effects. My hips feel like they're broken in a few places. I always refused a stunt double back in the day, and now I'm paying for it. *Damn.* The urgency to get to my apartment is now renewed.

Two hours later, we pull up to the Bole apartments. I park the car in the visitor's area and wake her up.

"Jay. We're here," I say, shaking her awake. "Come in and have a drink with me. I'll tell you all about life in LA."

"Sure. I'll bring my laptop. I want to know more about you. I'll write your bio."

By some miracle, my apartment is still mine. I thought I'd come back to nothing, homeless once again.

I tell her about life in Montana. I tell her about my parents and the hardship they went through to come to America. I tell her about how my mother died in the high hills during a snowstorm. I tell her about all the loves and broken hearts of my life. I tell her how it feels to be undesirable and burnt out. She's a curious lady and very kind…empathetic. She doesn't feel sorry for me. She takes me as I am.

After a few drinks and a mouth dry from talking, my stiff body pushes off the chair and I limp to my bathroom to run a hot bath. Before I jump in, I open my medicine cabinet looking for something to kill the pain. Not finished with undressing, I open the door and check on Jay. She's sitting at my dining room table fiercely typing away. The kid's got heart.

"Let it bleed, girl."

Chapter Three

The Heist

I've always hated my legs. I mean...I've worked on upper body and core strength my whole life, so while my upper half is still in pretty good form, it's too late for my bottom half. Fuck. White, hairy tree stubs. No, more like dying palm trees, and just when my bubble bath relaxes me, my nerves get shot again by just standing up and taking in the view.

What next?

I decide to dry off and use my towel to wipe my foggy mirror so I can shave. Considering all the years I've spent under the sun without protection, my skin has fared quite well. Two handsome wrinkles make an appearance every time I smile. *Character.* My razor is dull and well-used, and my bottle of shaving cream is empty, so I improvise and use my Pert to lather up my face. After a quick wash down, I admire my handsome Paul Newman face then decide to trim my eyebrows, only a bit. The last fixer-upper rehab tool is a quick dab of Old Spice, because who could resist that smell?

Out of the jailbird stripes and into my Wranglers and white T-shirt. I feel fresh, hip, like a new man hot and ready to slay the world.

I hesitate to open the door. Why can't I open my own damned bathroom fucking door? I need a beer.

"Hey."

"Hi. Oh! You look good. The stripes weren't working for you," she says, laughing, "but your zipper is down, dude."

"It's broke. Like me."

"I got us some grub. Boy, you must like to bath. You were in there a long time." She laughs again. *So happy*. My eyes turn toward the bags of groceries.

A case of beer, a pack of smokes, pizza, chips, fruit. Is that a bag of oats? *Holy fuck*... She's a health nut like the rest of the dames in this city.

"Did that hot bath help?"

"Oh yeah it did. Thanks."

Just as we started to chow down the damn lights went out. "Should have paid my utility bill I guess."

"Shit happens." She laughs.

"Did you at least get to charge your laptop?"

"Yes. It's good to go."

"What are you writing?"

"A short story, but my main jam is screenwriting. I'm working on a piece, but I may rewrite it a little bit."

"Since you met me?" I ask her, curious, but she doesn't answer.

We spend the entire day mostly in the dark talking about our pasts. She really listens. She asks lots of questions. She laughs and laughs. We get along pretty good.

After a few beers, I light up a smoke and start to relax, reflecting on everything which led me here today. Just a week ago, I walked into the prison and gave up. Two days ago, I thought I was going to die. For the first time in a long time the regret starts playing in my thoughts like a skipping record. If I had known then what I know now, what difference would it make?

"John. Do you have any candles? I can hook you up with some cash tomorrow to reconnect your utilities," Jay whispers, but I barely hear her. "Johnny?"

Guisy looks out my tiny living room window, pensively, and notes the bright pink sunset. I watch as she gets up and walks slowly into my living room and admires the photos on my walls, mostly stills from my movies. She finds an ashtray and butts her smoke.

Ready and willing to leave my torments behind for at least one evening, I reach out to this girl. What an awkward pair we make. I'll give her a chance even though my luck is fucked—because I need a friend. The room begins to fade into dark and our silhouettes meet at the coffee table. I take her hands and lift them up between us. Her hair is messy and wild. Her black eyeliner and mascara have melted away creating a raccoon mask around her eyes, smudged by the humidity, heat and alcohol, but her light heart smudges away my shame sitting heavy on my shoulders like boulders. Her goofy, buzzed grin and grunge out eyes match my torn jeans and stained Stanfield tee.

I tilt her head up, lift Jay's arm up high, and twist her wrist, spinning her gently around in a circle. Buzzed, she hesitates then giggles. I take a risk and fall into her arms as she dips me across her chest. Buzzed, I lose my balance and grab hold of her shoulders; tiny shoulders that can hold us both up just when I needed it the most. In her arms, I rise to my feet and, lost in hope, our faces touch. She takes a chance and looks up into my eyes. We're like two tired superheroes, and after a lengthy battle against the villains, I wrap my arms around her tightly.

Chapter Four

Higher

At last, I can feel without giving in to the fear. I've gone down far enough, can't get any lower. Yeah, I made *the* mistake and it fucked me royally, but I'm here in the now. I can breathe. I can start over again.

She feels so good, like a little bundle of joy, a newborn babe. So, I'll keep her in my arms, and when I let go, all that shit is shattered, fucking gone.

I'm torn, though. What to do? Man, she gives me chills all over. I can barely handle it. Not the horny kind of crap, something different…Like, can I kiss a nun? If I do, will I burn? Will I melt?

I'm already melted.

Ç

As broken as he is, is that a reflection of me? Are we a match of messed up? Does this make me as sad as him or as resilient?

I've overcome so much shit just to get here. I left the reservation in hope of living a life filled with my hopes...active, real dreams. My past has been horrific. Just thinking about how I was raised gives me chills that will best any horror flick I'll ever see. But I was the little train that could. After quitting school, I upgraded and got my grade twelve. Then I learned to write with heart and soul. It took years to accomplish all the little stuff...poverty, no food, second-hand clothes, surrounded by drunks and drugs.

No, I can't go back. I can handle failing because that just fuels me to try harder, to learn and do better. I think being an Indian in the city is going to be rough on me, but maybe this is my sanctuary too? Maybe, together, John and I can rise.

I've been walking on my knees all my life. Then I wobbled but learned to walk. I ran through all the shit, giving the bird to my past, and now I'm here. I made it and just when I needed a friend, a confidant, I ran into him, literally.

But are we friends? *What is this?*

He doesn't seem to mind I'm a native woman. He's like a homeless puppy: color blind, loyal and needing a home. I don't want him to let me go. This feeling is new for me. I've learned to embrace uncertainty because at least I can control that. So, what about the butterflies in my belly fluttering around nudging me, moving me, at his touch?

Chapter Five

Pure

"Hey, are you rich or something, casino money from the reservation, gold in those hills?" I ask.

"No." She tenses her shoulders as she tries to get comfortable on my loveseat. "Do you need more money?"

"Why, yes. I could use a little help with something personal."

"Personal? Like Botox or something?"

"Sure. That's it."

"Well, I have some money put aside. I am financing my own film. But yes, I do have liquid assets in my accounts. I've written a screenplay and, as a matter of fact, I'm looking for a male to fill a role. You might actually be a fit... Considering your background in the profession, do you want to look at my lead's lines?"

"Sure. So, let me get this straight. You're an 'indie going indie' and you need me? Sounds like you've searched for the perfect fit."

"I've done a little searching. The role doesn't pay much, to be honest. No union or agent needed. And it's a short drama set here in LA. I can help you out a bit to get you on your feet, plus I can draft out a contract for you to sign and I'll make payment arrangements too."

She's so naïve but no one else has my back. "Sure. Do you have your own place?"

"Yes."

"How about you crash here tonight, and we can start tomorrow."

"Ok. We'll settle in the morning. Bills, contracts, then the gym and we can shop around for a beauty treatment for you. Oh, and can you help me find an address tomorrow? There's a business I want to check out."

"Sure. I can do that. You get the couch."

"OK."

"Can I take your laptop to bed and read over your script?"

"Sure. Here, take it with you. Be honest and critique it too," says Guisy, passing me her laptop. "I'm pooped out, so good night." Jay pulls her tunic off and stretches her arms out. Then she ties her wild hair up into a double bun, looks at me and smiles right big, all dimply and cute. For a split second, I feel my chest start to pound—either my conscience or the pizza starting to say hello. Just when I'm almost ready to fake niceness she moves up to me, stares at me all serious then she gives me a massive hug.

"Thanks, John. I really need a friend."

As soon as I hear her snore, I open documents on her PC. *Damn. It's hot in here. Here's an interesting file.* It's her bank balance saved on her desktop. She's loaded. She must have a rich boyfriend or something. I wonder if she's a heavy sleeper.

I think I'll look for her purse.

Ϛ

Saturday was busy. We shopped for clothes and Jay picked up some summer dresses and even got her hair done up with streaks and foils. Then we went looking for records and rummaged through boutiques and bookstores searching for cool finds. After, she brought me back to her apartment so she could pick up her gym clothes.

While she worked out, I went to my spa appointment and took in the painful delights of needles, shiatsus and even got my eyebrows waxed and trimmed to get back to Hollywood ready, though all this was a first for me. We agreed on meeting at a local market to pick up more groceries for my place, and when we got back to my apartment, Jay pulled out her credit card, called up my utilities account and hooked up my bill. Voila—we had lights.

"Did you draft a contract?" I asked fully knowing she didn't have time.

"No. Sorry. I forgot but thank you for reviewing my script and giving me such honest feedback. I'm glad you're interested. You won't regret working with me."

She said 'with'! I've always been told 'for'. Starting to feel the guilt again, I decide to cut it off and ask her where she wanted to go and why this place was obviously so important to her.

"I need to go to 10175 Slater Avenue." She gleams with excitement. That face. God, she really is beautiful.

"What's the name of the business?"

"Southern California Indian Center!" she sings.

Oh boy. "Let's go. I know the area. Leave your car. We'll take a bus." Jay bustles around my apartment cleaning up and washing down the kitchen counters, fluffing the throw pillows on my couch and then grabs her toothbrush and toothpaste out of her purse and rushes to the bathroom. Singing as she brushes, she stops to mumble out to me, "I'm so excited! Thank you."

After a quick trip on the bus, I open the door to the center and curtly wave her in through the entrance.

"The smell of fried bread is just what I needed! I miss my momma's cooking," says Guisy. "Come on. Let's go say hi to the people at the canteen." Almost running like a doe, she shimmies herself into the lineup.

"Two bannocks please!"

"That will be ten dollars," the clerk tells Jay, but then addresses me with a gesture. I furrow my eyebrows but decide to pull out my debit card and give it a good old try.

"Declined," says the elder before returning her attention to Guisy. "Honey, where you from?"

"I'm from a small reservation just east of Seattle."

"You come here looking to be a movie star or something?" the Granny asks the girl with endearing emotion and concern. She looks up at me and frowns.

"Something like that," Guisy replies. "I'll try my card. I'm dying for a little piece of home."

"Oh no honey, this is on me." The elder lifts her aged hands out, one bearing a basket of warm fried bread dripping with butter, while the other gently moves forward, hesitates then reaches out for the young writer's face. "Honey, you stay as long as you want. If you need anything, you come see us here at this center. This is home for you now. You stay and enjoy a hot meal and a cup of tea."

"Thank you." Guisy blushes but takes in the gentle Grandmother's touch. The affection has me feeling a little out of sorts.

"You like it here, don't you?" I uncomfortably murmur, avoiding eye contact with my girl.

"Yes. This is just what I needed. A connection."

We sit down to eat, and with the music been played by the drummers thrumming in the background, she recalls her last visit with her family before she left for the awards night in Hollywood.

I relish her glowing demeanor and, most of all, her virtue. What surprised me most, however, was when she got up and cleaned all the dining room tables, swept the floors, and then emptied out the garbage and recycling stations, only to be called upon by the leader of the drum group. She looked up at me and smiled.

She was a beauty in my eyes, but tonight, I saw something else in her. I was learning about the unspoken words her people spoke. I witnessed the ease of communication between strangers in a different land yoked together by creed.

When I heard her singing the traditional pow-wow song, it shook me deep down inside. I lowered my head, sitting alone in the corner with the last piece of fried bread. Fidgeting was my response. I forced my hands into my new coat pockets.

But then I was reminded why I was with her in the first place: an envelope I took from her satchel. It was marked with a dollar sign and it felt thick enough to set me up, yet thin enough she wouldn't miss it.

Chapter Six

Hard core

We parted ways. I, the reluctant one, but I did it. I needed to chill and grab a few drinks. I needed to shove these fucked up feelings somewhere...*anywhere* to eradicate the shit flying around in my head, damn it.

It's her eyes; pure and happy. They don't judge me.

I decided to walk down the boulevard to find something to do and it was the guitar riffs and smashing symbols that caught my attention. When I got to the entrance, I stopped to check out my reflection in the tinted-out windows and *damn*, I liked what I saw. I still look hot. I look like I did ten years ago...only better.

So, I lit a smoke and then checked my cell. She texted me and thanked me for a wonderful day. She saved a picture she took of us and put it on the front of my phone—not sure how she did it, but I like it. She made me smile and my curiosity made my thumb smooth over her picture, but it was the singer in the bar that brought me back to reality.

I've got money to blow.

Blow...

I won't do that, but everything else is a go tonight. When I walked into the bar I felt right at home. Old school pool tables, old school music, bitches wearing leather with their hair teased, easing my swagger on. Right away a hot blonde came to my side wanting to dance. We danced, and danced, and laid down shot after shot of Mr. Daniel's.

She treated me like a god. She kept on going to the bathroom and coming out excited and hyper to see me. That's all it took to make me want to bring her home. And that I did. That night was a royal fuck fest—wild, like how I used to be. She was rough on me, but she wanted it back.

Ç

Girl, get a grip.

Standing in front of my mirror I stare myself down. "You can do it, Guisy. You can do it," I mumble to myself. I'm just too excited. I want to go see him. I want to go over my production binder for my film. I need his ideas. Brainstorming with him will help. Besides, I left my laptop at his place. *If only he'd answer a text.* Darn his ass, he probably doesn't know how to. He's probably still up. I'll cab it there since I left my car there too.

His door is open. *I'll just knock and go in. He's probably up.* I hear music. *He's up!* I'm so excited.

"Hello, John? It's Guisy. I picked up a bottle of my favorite wine. Hello?"

No answer.

"Hello? Johnny, where's your wine glasses? "I search a cupboard and find them. "John, you're too quiet. You alive, dude?" Glasses in hand, I push his bedroom door open.

"Get up old man." I giggle, but he's nowhere to be seen. "What are you doing? Are you hiding?" *Where the hell is he?* Then I hear a door open behind me.

"Jay? Jay, what the hell are you doing here?" John slurs. Behind him stumbles in a tall, naked blonde dripping wet from an apparent tryst for two in the shower.

"Oh. Shit. That didn't take you long to...whatever. Sorry for bothering you." I straighten my ruffled coat, lift my chin up and push John aside, making my way past his bimbo.

"Guisy! Stay. She's leaving," he pleads behind me.

"Fuck off!"

John throws the blonde her clothes and then leads her out the door by her elbow, barging in front of me. He turns around.

"Why you mad, girl?" he asks, confused as he puts on his leather vest and slips his watch on.

"Where are my car keys?"

"Is that wine for us?"

I grab the bottle of wine and start to pour it down the kitchen drain.

"What a waste, fucking stop that," he says, trying to grab the bottle from my hand. I let it fall into the sink with a crash, then turn to leave.

"Where are you going, Jay?" asks John.

"Home, I'm going home."

"Why?"

I turn around and meet his eyes. "I know you took my money. That was my first draw needed for site rental and payment to my production staff." An angry tear crevasses my cheekbone revealing my pain.

"You knew, and you didn't say anything to me?"

"I figured you must have really needed it, but the thing is…if you had asked, I would've given it to you."

"Who the fuck does that kind of shit?"

"John. I never entered this world with money and when I leave my pockets will be empty. Goodbye."

"I'm sorry. Look, I'll grab it. I'll give it back. I'm sorry, Jay. I mean it." John scurries around looking through the suit jacket he must have worn earlier in the evening. "Damn. I can't find it. Help me look for it, Jay." Panicking he shuffles over the table knocking empty beer bottles on the floor and dumping his ashtray all over the place. He runs into his bedroom and turns on the light with renewed sobriety. I can see it in his eyes.

It's the kind of sober one gets when they fuck up bad. The money is nowhere to be found.

John slowly comes to the same realization that I've already come to—that he was ripped off. "You mad?"

"I'm disappointed."

"I'm sorry."

"I know."

"What can I do?"

"I'll be okay," I respond. I get up, ash my cigarette in the tray on the floor, and walk out the door.

I want to have hope in my aged movie star. I want to have hope in my dreams. Hell...I've been fucked over before and bounced back every time, but this time feels different. This time I'm wiped out.

I just need to be home in my bed to think things through. There's always a way. I was born with resilient bones building me up.

But why do I feel so fucking alone?

Chapter Seven

Reservation

"Guisy. If you're going to stay here, then you have to get a job. You hear me girl?"

"Yes, Auntie."

My back is sore from sleeping on the floor. The small window of the reservation box house has no curtain or blinds, and it lets in tiny sunbeams which creep across the sheet reminding me of the total desolation I was born into and was bred for.

"I knew you'd make us all look bad chasing your big dreams. Get over yourself and join the club."

"Yes, Auntie." Even the Rezz dog and bourgeoisie fat cat in the corner of my bedroom glance over at me like I'm shit— dirtier than their own. They reinforce my aunt's rants, like they know I'm a failure, as immaterial as the tattered blanket on the dilapidated floor.

"The Boot is looking for a driver for deliveries. Go see her. Tell her I sent you. You got my car still, doncha?"

"Yes, Auntie." I picture myself driving my old station wagon filled with beer, whiskey and moonshine, shaking every nut and bolt of her jalopy as I drive down the narrow gravel potholed road around my reservation like a zealous Bible thumper going door to door. I would save countless souls, bottle in hand.

It was at that point I gave up.

ς

I walked and walked every day. Eventually running became easy. My liver was given a fresh start. I might not have been working, but I'd get up every day like I was heading to a gig.

I exhausted every contact and 'friend' in search of a role— anything, a commercial even. Failure at the back of my mind, I would come home and if my body began to shake and nudge me to give in, I would fill a bucket up with warm soap and water and destroy any morsel of dust, dirt, and cigarette grime off my walls. Then, I would shower and head to bed, thankful for another day.

Hands in pocket I walked to the transit bus and headed out. 'Where the Creator leads me, I will follow,' I remember hearing Jay say. It made me smile when she said that because she believed it. So that's just what I did. I missed her.

On the bus, I texted Guisy again and again, but she didn't answer me. *I won't give up on her, ever.*

The bus stopped, and I felt the urge to jump off, so I did and there on the side of the transit station was a big sign; a beautiful, green, lush sign: "Friends of the Los Angeles River."

I'm going to see if I can volunteer with these guys. I think it's meant to be.

I made some new kind of friends, people that did things for good and for no apparent reason other than making a difference for their community. I enjoyed it. I helped market their Great LA River Clean Up and did the grunt work they needed, sifting through the vast, used-up concrete and colonized river for garbage and helping dispose of all types of trash. I was humbled. What we have done to the land and to the first people is a tragedy in so many ways.

But something still bugged me. It wasn't her. It wasn't missing her. It was the fact I stole from a friend. I had to make things right or I knew I couldn't keep going on like this. So, I caught a ride back to my apartment and ran in to get a key.

"Where do you have to go now, John?" asks one of my cleanup crew peeps.

"To my storage locker, I've got to see my baby."

It was the one thing that meant the most to me in the whole entire world. My ride: the Harley Davidson Knucklehead.

I called an old friend—a film industry golden boy producer.

"Hey. Remember when you wanted to buy my Knucklehead?"

"John? Shit, I thought you were dead," he says and laughs.

"I was."

"How much?" asks the producer.

Playing it cool, ready for a battle, but giving no room for negotiation I say, "A hundred G's and I'll throw in the coat and helmet."

"That's a real bargain," the producer responds.

I wince. The pain of losing my baby is like a dagger in the heart. But the loss of Jay's friendship hurts even more. Not only did I steal from her, I know I crushed her dream and took what she needed to start up her project. And I know how hard it is for a Native American to break out as a writer, producer, or anything else in the industry. It was already hard enough. I want her to succeed and this is one of the ways I knew I could pay her back.

Balls to the wall: I call my girl. No more texting—pissing around. I'm going to find her and bring her back.

Chapter Eight

Undoing

"Ma...there's a white boy here!"

"Really?" She walks to the screen door with her hands on her hips, looking me up and down. For the first time in my life, I'm speechless.

I take off my baseball cap and decide to come on strong. "I'm looking for Guisy. The people at the casino said she lived down the end of the long dirt road, which led me here. Does she stay here, ma'am?"

I can't breathe. I've never been on a native reservation before, but I have nothing to lose.

My eyes dart around the living room searching for her face or evidence that she's been here. The walls host an array of photos and wall hangings depicting a fallen native warrior riding a lamed horse. School photos of varied children and teenagers hang precariously above an old couch with no legs. An old school television is the stand for a smaller TV and on top of that sits a tired looking antenna. A tattered sheet covers part of the living room window, which is jarred open hosting a fan, filling the room with more warm air.

My nose twitches. I can't get over the scent of lavender trees blossoming on each side of the porch. It's a juxtaposition to everything else I'm seeing. Swinging from the ceiling fan in front of me are several fly sticks swarmed with the carcasses of the dead hovering around and around and around. *The Enquirer* sits on the coffee table as well as an ashtray and several open cola cans with ash around the rims.

Finally, I understand her infirmity: poverty and lack surround her. Guisy couldn't really live here, could she?

"Why? What do you want with her?" she barks. Her presence shows no endearment for my Guisy. She looks agitated. She cracks her knuckles and bulges her brown eyes at me waiting for an answer.

"I'm her friend. Oh, and I work for her. That's why I'm looking for her." My hands rest high up on the screen. I'm about to get in her face to get a direct answer until I see a little girl walk up behind the woman, tugging at her healthy frame. My eyes soften, and my throat gets filled with emotion. She's such a cute little thing…a miniature little Jay.

"If she's not home, could you tell me where I could find her? I travelled a long way to see her." Getting nowhere, I decide to turn on the charm to get my way. I widen my big brown eyes and bat my lashes a few times giving her the most charming smile. My palms open to her showing I mean no harm. Unspoken gestures speak volumes.

"I'm her aunt." This time she smiles back in response. She relaxes her arms by her side and pouches her lips together. I watch this—her reaction to my attention—and she softens and becomes helpful. She points her lips in the direction of the casino.

"She's at the Indian casino?" I ask, excited.

"No! And it's called the *Native American* casino, by the way. Guisy's working in town somewhere serving, I think. There're only a few places open, try there. Or if you want you can come in and wait."

"If you don't mind." She opens the door and invites me in.

"You want to put your bag in her room?"

"Yes please." My dimples dance. I'm excited to see where Jay sleeps.

"Down the hall, last door on the left." I nod and go down the hall over piles of toys and scattered clothes and diapers, some of them used. I can barely stand the smell but decide to put on a happy face and breathe with my mouth. The door handle to Jay's room is broken so I push it open gently.

True to Jay's nature, the room is clean and sparse. No pictures hanging, but there is evidence of tacks and tape strewn like a constellation everywhere. The window has a curtain. Her clothes are neatly piled in the corner of the bedroom. I place her laptop and charger down gently on her makeshift bed on the floor. Though it hurts my knees, I kneel and run my hand down the two sheets with a pillow on top that constitutes her bed. It's sad; a far cry from what she left in LA, though her blanket is a beautifully designed aboriginal quilt probably handmade just for her.

I feel I can't wait any longer, my longing for my friend runs deep. Without a word, I quickly run out of the house and make my way back into the local town.

Twenty minutes later, I'm searching through every shop window. Most restaurants are closed. So, I walk into a hotel hoping there might be a restaurant or coffee shop open but nope, nothing. I find my way back to the main street and walk until I hear music, loud music. A bar!

I wouldn't mind having a couple drinks and maybe some food. My rumbling stomach and my need for an ice-cold draft nudges me through the doors. Three drink max. That's my new rule.

I'm bewitched by the open kitchen showing all the cooks and prep staff cheffing up a storm. *For a rundown place they sure have a great diner.* I search the walls for weekly specials and find a menu pinned close to the till. I make my order and decide to look around for a table, so I can hopefully call Guisy and tell her I am here to see her.

My attention is diverted by the loud roar of men hollering and whistling behind me, though I can't see them. I watch as my beer on a tray comes my way, and when the waitress arrives, I ask for a glass of water too, water then beer, water then beer. I had a new routine and wouldn't be sidetracked or weakened, but I couldn't deny that I still loved the taste of an ice cold frosty. My burger arrives and I dig in.

There they go again. They must be watching a baseball game. I turn around and make my way to the group huddling around a large table. The DJ blasts a familiar song. I've heard it before but can't place it. I stand behind the group and lift my burger to my mouth. I peer over the crowd of men sitting beside the stage. *What the fuck?* But what I see next blows my mind. I can't even take a bite...there's a stripper starting to dance.

"Fuck me!"

She stumbles to the center of the stage. Fumbling with her buttons, she stops walking then works each one until they're undone. The men start to boo her. She tries to walk all sexy but it's obvious she can't walk in three-inch heels. Her knees knob together, and she falls on her ass. Pissed, she gives them the bird and whips her coat off throwing it at the crowd. The stripper taps her ass, and they roar and whistle, shouting, "Take it off! Take it off!" which she does. She wiggles out of her short shorts and throws it at the pole behind her. Slowly she lies back on her elbows and shakes her body to the beat.

When money gets thrown at her she moves her legs tight to each other and lifts them up into the air, then spreads her legs apart like she's done it a million times. The stripper then rolls on her belly and brings her butt up into the air wiggling backwards towards the men. She whips her hair out of her ponytail and slings it around in circles. She turns to the crowd and licks her high-glossed, painted, electric-pink lips. It's when she stands up and starts making her way to the pole that I drop my burger. The tattoo on her shoulder gives it away first, but then she takes off her pink, glittered, bejeweled mask and ripped pink tank top.

I drop my beer and burger to the ground. Glass shatters.

Chapter Nine

Cyborg

My head feels like it's going to explode. I'm so mad at her. Mad at all the pukes watching her like she's some mindless twit spreading her legs for the world to see. So, I do what I have to do.

Pulling her off the stage, by her legs, was easy. Pushing her into the men's john was easy. Holding my hand up and flinging it at her face, well that was easy too. The hard part was stopping mid-air and bridling my rage. I failed at that.

I grab her by her neck. Time slows down as if I'm idling in my car, bottlenecked on the hellish 405 Freeway, overheating with no air conditioning.

Why would she give it away and why was that bloody familiar?

"Can you get your stinking old hands off me?" Guisy's ready to knee me in the junk. I see it in her eyes—a woman crossed. That old familiar fear realized steadies my hands until I'm able to breathe and let her go.

"Man. The men's washroom is way cleaner than the women's. Un-freaking believable!" she says, looking around the dilapidated cubical as she takes in the unfamiliar scent of sanitary cubes sitting all blue in each urinal.

I take off my jacket and pass it to Guisy. "Here, cover yourself up."

"You cover yourself up," she says as the bathroom door flings open. The owner of the bar stands in front of her and taps his finger on her forehead. A few more drinks and I would have decked the motherfucker for doing that.

"You're fired." He turns and leaves the way he came.

"Good riddance," I say, meaning it.

"I needed that job, John!" she yells, glaring at me as she rummages through her purse and pulls out a pack of menthols and her lighter. I follow as she walks down the back alley between the strip club and the hotel.

I can't answer her. I can't shake the damned feeling— emotions…damned emotions.

"What are you doing here?" she asks me as she inhales a drag of her cigarette, not even bothering to wipe away the rain drops on her face gaining a stormy momentum.

"I was passing through."

"Did you go to my house?"

"Is that what you'd call it?" I grunt.

"Yeah," she responds aggressively.

"Guisy. Come back to the city. You're burning out here. It's been four months and look how far down you've gotten yourself."

"Is that what you think, asshole?"

"You're staying in a dump. You're shoving your tits around and wiggling your ass for a dollar bill. What would you call that?"

"That dump is all I got so fuck off."

"I will," I whisper.

She looks at me, resigned. "Let's go for a drink."

"Sure."

We walk into the hotel pub and sit down at the bar. She orders shots and doubles. When she orders more rounds, I push the glasses away and ask for water. She eyes me, confused.

"You've changed." I ignore her comment.

"Let's get a room and get you cleaned up."

And we do. After a long shower, Guisy enters the suite wearing long johns and a T-shirt. Her face is pink from all the scrubbing she had to do to take off the stage makeup. She empties her backpack to find her makeshift wallet which hoarded all her tips and strip bills and coins. Along with the baggie, she pulls out her dollar store notebook—aka her ledger—and opens it up to her last entry. Tonight's storehouse totals $315.72. Not a bad fix for tonight's short show. Still, it pisses me off.

"That money is so gross, Guisy."

"For your goddamn fatherly information...I don't strip all the way. If I did, I would make more money, but I could never do that."

"Oh." I'm surprised, but not. I start to relax knowing she protected herself.

"I need to chill. Let's watch one of your movies to take my mind off the choking thing you did to me." Guisy grabs her tablet and the remote. She scrolls through YouTube and finds several titles. "What should we watch?"

"Whatever." Nervous, I start to worry about which one she will pick, hoping the infamous, wretched title from my past won't display on the feed. She picks one and fiddles with the remote, streaming it to the television. Confused, I ignore her, crack my knuckles, and force my eyes closed. *If she finds it and watches it... it will kill me.*

I was desperate! I didn't know that falling into that horrible trope would kill my career.

I took the role of a child killer. It wrecked me as an actor and a man. No one would cast me after that. Who could blame them? *She will think I am so freaking low. I can't do this. I can't face the shadows of my past again.*

"I'm going to shower. My bones are aching from the cold wet weather here."

"Sure. You stink."

"You stink," I mumble back to her before shutting the bathroom door. I turn on the shower and slowly undress. I look in the mirror, admiring my now clearly defined abs. My face is contoured and chiseled like it used to be when I was young and fit.

Still, I can't shake the fucked-up feeling in my stomach. Shame is a bitch.

In the shower I start to get dizzy, so I hold myself up by gripping the wall below the shower head, allowing the stream of hot water to pour down the back of my neck. My chest tightens up, and the only way I can breathe is by clenching my jaw tight and grinding my teeth.

I made the biggest mistake of my life with that movie, and it's still following me. I'm forever fucked. When I walk out of this bathroom the one person that sees me as human will look at me like I'm shit, I know it.

She's probably watching it now. Fuck that shit. She's a little puke and I'm here to make things right because that's what I do. I'll pay her back and be on my way. *But if she hurts me, I know I'll go ballistic.*

When I hear her banging on the bathroom door, I open my eyes and allow the water to flow over my face, and my mouth takes in the bleached-out water and spits it out. My heart rate starts to steady, and my shoulders stop hunching, releasing all the stress that even the hot current of water couldn't rescind. As I step out of the shower, I flex my leg muscles and my chest. When the towel drops to the floor, I decide I'm done. I look up. Gently yet methodically I wipe away the steam building on the mirror. My body still and poised, I open my eyes. I force myself to reflect on the role I once took.

I'm safe. Breathe out the shit, breathe in the good.

Chapter Ten

Cartography

"It's like all I deserve is shit!" Jay cries into the wind, leaning against the broken rails of the hotel balcony. Her fingers race to text her Aunt back while slipping on her runners.

Ϛ

I knew I had to deal with my Settler response to my other half who happens to be Indigenous. So, as soon as my breath work brought me into my moment, I knew I had to run. I had to be outdoors.

This town is on the outskirt of Guisy's reservation, so finding a path to run on would be easy because I had to expand the time and space between the stressor and my reaction to take me out of my manly flight, fight, and freeze response. When I got back to the hotel room, the door was open. I knew something was wrong and I knew where Guisy would go.

She must be so mad at me. I gotta make things right! I raced back to the reservation. My intuition led me all the way.

Ç

Probably the only white man around...this could be dangerous, is all I could think as I walked by the dilapidated buildings and bare windows of the reservation. But what other choice do I have? I'll just give the kid the money I owe her, compound of course, and that will be that. I don't belong here.

Knock.

No answer.

Knock. Knock.

No answer.

Pounding, I start to worry.

"Let me in!" I yell through the screen door, shocked that there is nothing there to prevent the pouring rain from feeding the thin line of fungus mold parading in the cracks.

I open the door and look up at the alarm clock positioned vicariously on the floor beside the coffee table. It's dead. *Power must be out.* Making my way to her bedroom, I can't shake the feeling that I'm being watched. *I hope she's ok.*

I pass the first bedroom and peer inside. Empty. The bathroom door is open, the second bedroom vacant. The hallway floor creaks announcing my steps. I can barely breathe. Guisy's bedroom door is open, so I leap inside prepared to hold her or slap her for coming back here.

But it's empty.

"Shh," a soft scared voice whispers to me in desperation.

My skin is covered in gooseflesh, but I follow the voice into the final bedroom—the master—and slowly pull out my phone and turn on the flashlight app. There, crouched over and shivering is my Guisy, only she's not alone. She's holding two children in her arms.

"Sweet stuff, are you ok?" My whisper climbs over the lead lure lodged in my throat. I'm desperate to touch my friend.

She turns her head up and looks. When I see the blood trickling down over her forehead, pain rakes my chest. The lights flicker on and off, giving her the chance to stand up.

"John, I'm scared." I don't move to her. My eyes roll over the room until I find what I need: a child size baseball bat.

"Grab your stuff and let's go."

"Where are we going?"

"Back to LA." I pull out my phone.

"Who are you calling?" asks Guisy.

"I'm calling the cops."

"No."

"Why not?"

"Just don't."

"Guisy. That's what people do when there's violence in the home."

"Please don't," she repeats.

"There are children here. We need to get them to a safe place."

Her head sags. "I know. Ok." She grabs her satchel and pulls out a notebook, black and leatherbound.

"Why are you handing me this right now?"

"I've been documenting how many times and the dates my aunt has left my cousins alone. She takes off and comes back nuts."

"She needs professional help."

"I know. Now I have enough evidence to prove it. You can hand it to the police when they get here," says Guisy.

"Why me?"

She shakes her head. "I'm invisible, John. I'm invisible here in my own land and territory, but they will see you and take this serious."

I shake my head. "I can't."

"Say no to *her* then." She pulls her sheet over her shoulder revealing the little cutie I met when I first arrived on the Rezz. For four years old, she's tiny, but her eyes shine bright with hope at the weirdo standing above her like a porcelain giant.

We all walk down the hallway, ready to run down the long road to meet the police officers on their way, but then Guisy remembers all the money she's got stashed in her room.

"John, run back to my room and grab your bag, and my stash too. It's hidden under the vent cover."

"What kind of stash?"

"I've saved for the kids. They need clothes and stuff for when they start off at the lost-n-found."

Puzzled, I nod my head and run back to her room while Guisy fumbles along through the front room, kids in hand, eager to get out the door to safety.

I do a thorough search. "There's no money here!"

"I know. It's gone."

Chills run up over my back down my arms. I drop my bags to the floor. *Shit.*

"You two think you're so good that you could take my kids away? You're ruining my meal ticket, asshole. I need their government money. So now you're going to pay!" screams Guisy's angry aunt.

I step forward ready to bolt but lose my balance when my first step falls on the baseball bat. I fall, and when I look up, I get a brief glance at Guisy's aunt as she picks up the bat and hits my shoulder knocking me back to the ground. She shuffles to my side, so I whip my hands out, grip her wide ankles, and pull, bringing her down with me. I get up and run out the front door, following the running shadows in the distance. When I catch up, I fall into Guisy's open arms.

"Where are the police? I told them we needed them!" I say, looking back at the house.

"John, they don't come to the reserve."

A new kind of fear kicks my hope in the gut, but I'm a fighter. I dial 911. The police answer, but I don't even let them speak.

"I just called, so listen. One of two things could happen within the next ten seconds. A—you come out here to the reservation and save these two children. B—I'll video live everything and send it to the networks right now!" *Click.*

I whip my coat off and wrap it over the twins, giving them extra warmth and, I hope, reassurance. We hide just off Main Street, and when police cars, ambulances and even a fire truck drive past, I flag them down. After I hand them the leather-bound book with notes, Guisy steps in front of me and takes over. After a while, she rejoins me and the kids.

"Can we take them back to LA?" I ask.

"No. The culture shock would be too hard on them. But they're going to be ok now, John. They'll be staying with the band nurse. She's married to the cop. They'll stay with them at least until they can sort out a new living arrangement. Once my aunt is done treatment and does her time, maybe then my cousins can get settled back into real life with their mom."

"Wow babe, wow. You're amazing!"

"I'm not alone. I sent a message to our Chief. He is a good man. I asked him for help with this entire family," she says, sighing deep and shaking her head. "You see, childhood trauma is toxic and has been passed down through many generations of my family. I asked our Chief to hire the very best counselors for our community. He answered, and the Healing Centre in town are setting up an emergency response unit that can act as a mental health triage centre for children in need, pregnant moms, and stressed-out dads, to find help, hope, and an opportunity to take that trauma shit, name it, give it to Creator, then ask God Creator to turn it into fertilizer to bless this nation."

"Oh my God, you planned all this by yourself," I say, incredulous.

"I did. This is what I do. And now this is what you do too."

"What you do?"

"I help children."

"Why?"

"Because no one was there to help me."

ς

I wasn't sure if it was the freezing, frigid wind, or the rain, or just plain old shock, but something in this moment revealed the calamity Guisy was. The ambulance driver encouraged Guisy to go to the hospital to get checked over. She asked that the children be seen by a doctor first, then her. She asked me to ride in the ambulance with the children; she didn't want them to be alone.

A few minutes later, we arrive at the small hospital in town. Wanting to come clean, I hold her hand and sit her down on the hospital bed. "I came here to see you. I have enough money to get your movie going."

"What are you talking about?"

"And another thing, you've shown me the worst part of yourself and it makes you all the more precious to me. I'm going to do the same."

"Are you native too? My long-lost cousin tenth removed?" says Guisy with a snarky tone and chuckle.

"Nope, at least I don't think so." I pull her closer to my side. She's almost on my lap, so close I can smell her breath, feel her layers, her angel feathers.

Longing to hold her, I grab her hovering hands and bring them gently to my chest, lowering my head, and look into her eyes, asking permission. I plant one gentle kiss on her blushing palm, and in my eyes the maps of atrocity trickle away with my tears. The stripper jumps on my lap and hugs me tight, her wild black hair a mess everywhere.

"Oh, by the way, we've got to work on your script. It reads like a doc."

Smiling at my goofy doe-eyes she punches my shoulder.
"OK".

Chapter Eleven

Raison d'être

We spent precious time on the reservation at my family home. We ordered a garbage bin and filled it full of aged furniture, rotting groceries, soured clothes, and broken bed frames. The mattresses too said their goodbyes. We pulled the flooring up and bleached the naked floorboards beneath, grinding down the nails used to hold the musty carpet in place. John and I barely spoke. Instead, we worked hard pulling down all light fixtures which dangled vicariously like meat hooks in a butcher's walk-in. When the shack was all bones, we left, and went for a ride on the city bus to pick out paint, windows, and a furnace.

There's something magical about doing this renovation on our family home. Yeah, it feels good. I remember doing my homework, or more like trying to do my homework here. My auntie partied all night, my uncle passed out. It felt good to rip the broken light fixture down, remembering it hanging so low for most of my life.

Once, I daydreamed of hanging myself from it. Life was hard, but it was the hopelessness that was a bitter cold that never went away.

But I felt like I wasn't alone throwing that light fixture into the garbage bin; I felt my Creator healing my brokenness. The past served its purpose; cycles are broken. I am strong enough to cry now and strong enough to rebuild this home for the next generation, leaving them a great inheritance: hope.

Ç

I've seen a lot of dives in my time but this one takes the cake. To think this is the house she grew up in. This is the very epitome of who she is. It's heartbreaking. I've given her the space she needs because I sense the demons surfacing as she works and the brutal strength she bolsters, needs, in order to place all things where they rightfully belong: in the past piled up with the rest of the shit. Who knows what went on here? But judging from the lives of her little cousins, she probably had it worse.

I had no problem being the only white man hanging around her Rezz. And who would've thought that I would be accepted! Many neighbors and the curious passersby popped in as we worked, chatting amongst themselves. One elderly couple even set up a makeshift table below the cherry tree. They came by many times throughout the days bringing deer jerky, bannock, stew & rice, blackberry pies and homemade iced tea.

The old lady and I grew quite close, enough so that she would stand behind me as I inhaled her cooking. Then one day, she smiled at me and slowly her hand reached out for my head. Guisy said she wanted to feel my wavy, curly hair. She'd never touched a mane of fuzz before, or even a white person for that matter, so of course I took my baseball cap off, and at that moment, I looked up at her frail husband and noticed his long, white hair braided sitting under a western top hat. He must have been a catch in his day, and judging from the kindness flowing from this woman, she is too.

ς

He gave me my laptop and told me to rest. He told me he was going to fix my roof, pull up the shingles and replace the rotting wood as he held a roll of weather membrane. He told me to write a story, freestyle. No Avid. No blog. But to write that story down for my eyes only.

As I watched the community members bring bags of used clothes to him, I laughed... They think him poor, a vagrant. He smiled, and did the Indian nod before examining each shirt, boxer, sock and pant like he was opening Christmas presents under a towering, richly adorned tree. He was fitting in better than I could have ever imagined.

As he climbed up the ladder, I turned on the power to my laptop. As he began prying the tiles off in a horizontal line, I opened Word. With a coffee pot beside me and a pack of cigarettes in my pocket, my fingers hovered over each letter wondering where to start.

I remembered the teachings of my grandparents. I took a cigarette out of the package. I pinched the filter off, then lifted the broken cigarette up to the sun. I closed my eyes and gave thanks, gratitude, out loud, talking to Creator. I laid the tobacco down on to the earth as an offering—my sacredness.

I wrote about this journey. I started smoking in grade seven— as soon as I hit puberty and my aunt started hitting me. Tobacco is a sacred medicine—well it used to be to my people. They say tobacco has a spirit and that every spirit has a job. I think tobacco spirit chose me as its job. I think it laid its life down as an offering to make sure that I live, that I would never commit suicide. I think it protected me.

The home makeover took several months to complete. Even the very foundation had to be reinforced. We shoveled a ditch around the perimeter of the shack, mixed cement in a barrow and poured it between new forms. The septic tank was pulled out and replaced.

When it was finally complete, I decided to look in the mirror. I no longer looked tired. I no longer have dim sclera— healing whitened that thin, tough layer. My black pupils are sweet like licorice.

I spin around like the ballerina on my jewelry box, but instead of a white flowing dress, I'm dressed in buckskin wearing an ornate, braided, cedar bark crown.

"I've been here many times in the last two months. What is going on? There was no mention why you have changed the layout of this house?" says Chief Clem. Perplexed, he walks up to us.

"Guisy. Why do you have every bedroom set up for a child? Why are there two home offices? What is going on?"

"John and I have rebuilt this house, and we've paid off the remaining mortgage," I reply.

"You're moving back?" The Chief stares at me, his joy transparent.

"Nah. This is now the new home for Children and Families. Here is the key," I say, beaming as I hand him the key. "Please run programs in this building that will reinforce the safety and nurturing of all children in need—the unborn, the infants, the children, the teens, the young parents and, most of all, those hurting parents who need help to become what they were meant to be—healthy, and full of our culture and our lost traditions."

Chief Clem was beside himself.

"Thank you Guisy, and you too, John. I know and understand the great loss you have gone through. I see you healing, both of you, and I hope to lift you up in ceremony and prayer. My home is your home. I will take care of this family including their mother and all extended family members. May Creator bless you on your journey."

Chapter Twelve

Grand Slam!

Living here in Los Angeles is outrageous. It's nothing like home on the Rezz. When I returned, I sought out the familiar because that's what we do. Every step I take I'm walking in two worlds: the left so conscious and aware of technology, busy streets, working for the almighty dollar, and the right cognizant of the zealous Creator who gives me breath on borrow until my next journey, giving gratitude to my relations past, Mother Earth below my feet and Father Sky above. It hasn't been easy to get to this point, but I'm not the first or the last.

I reflect on my past, on my torrid childhood and the trauma I've endured and emulated, and I've created a decree of emancipation. All during the human horrors, Creator upheld me, kept me alive—I was never truly alone.

Granny taught me to forgive and Mama taught me to love hard, laugh hard. I've embraced the good, the bad, the ugly, and the beautiful, not letting that define the lady in the mirror. I'm like the acquitted vampire girl—different by nature, but bearing a daylight ring on her toe that gives her the opportunity to ravage life under the bright Sun. The blinds no longer blackout the windows of my 'home' and now I am free to sow my Creator-given gifts. It's what I do with this life I've being given that defines me. Resilience is my crown.

Chapter Thirteen

Come In, the Door's Unlocked

My plans for tonight are cleaning up my pad, paying my bills online, following up with my notifications, and the three S's. Guisy texted "what's up" and I told her "2001" and she didn't answer or complain so I know she's coming over. She's a die hard. I'm sure she has a copy of the script and I've got the movie. It's Monday. We do this every Monday. It's our time. Nothing gets in the way. She'll never expect what I'm brewing tonight!

When the doorbell rings, I bolt to the door and answer it. I've got a question for my babe. I have my momma's ring, her wedding ring. Tonight is the night I propose.

Ç

I knock gently at his door grinning, my hands holding the prize: theatre popcorn with extra butter, a bag of licorice, and a two liter of cola. Inside my jacket, against my chest, sits my special gift for my best friend. He lets me in.

"Hey sugar-face, I missed you!"

"I missed you too...you brought your onesie? I thought these went out of style at the age of three."

"Relax. I brought you something too."

"Oh no way, I'm not wearing baby clothes."

I can't get over how smashingly great he looks. A bit weathered but he pulls it off so well.

"What? Why are you staring at me like that?" he asks.

"No reasons other than you need these." I lift out a pair of socks from her bag.

"Those are fucking ugly," he says, though seconds later, he pulls on the striped toes.

"Come on. Let's start. We can share the script as we watch the movie."

"What is it tonight?"

"*9 1/2 Weeks*. It's a classic." I jump on his couch and pour the soda before pulling off my T-shirt. Once I slip into my onesie, I zip it all the way to the top and slide across his solid wood floor.

"You're a nut! What about *2001: A Space Odyssey*? It's our favorite." He grabs my hand and pulls me down onto the couch.

"No. Go make popcorn, then we'll begin," I reply.

"Guisy, I missed you." He grabs my wild long hair and wraps it around his hand, tugging me to his chest. For a moment, I peer up at his dimpled face and without a thought, I kiss him on his chin then slap his ass for good measure.

"Food now please and thank you," I grunt out and push him into the kitchen.

ς

We play nice, friendly, and platonic, until Guisy gets tired, plops her pillow on my lap and snuggles into me, her bestie, arm entangled around my leg. My hand relaxes on her pigtail, smoothing it over and, occasionally, I lift it up to my nose and take in her fresh scent. I smile and close my eyes in bliss.

Then I made the move. I eye up Guisy's curves that couldn't hide under her dorky outfit, the flannel so soft and pink bringing out the beauty of her skin tone. Unfettered, my hand moves up and down over her outline and I hope for a reaction from her. I get one. She snuggles deeper into my embrace, and I'm in heaven.

When she starts to snore, I smile again and close my eyes. I don't mind that her sinuses make vulgar sounds, and I don't mind the fact she was drooling in her sleep. I accept her just like she accepts me.

She shifts and turns her body over. The pillow slips from under her and lands on the floor, waking her up. Naturally, she opens her big tired brown eyes. I lift one supporting knee up and bring her into my full view.

God she's cute even with sleep gathering around her eyes and popcorn shells napping on her neck.

I move my hand under her chin to shoo them away and she smiles. She stops my hand and holds it long enough for me to read the little crazy thoughts rolling around in her head, and she clarifies it when she takes my hand and leads it to the onesie zipper and top button. My hand stalls, but Guisy, the brave one, takes the risk and unbuttons it, biting her bottom lip.

"Guisy. Not here," I say, making her frown. I love her so much it breaks my heart. I never want her to feel unwanted or unappreciated, and while I've never made the move, I can't get her out of my mind; not that I ever tried to.

I slowly stand up and make my way to the bedroom.

"Babe, come here," I whisper, turning around to see my girl.

Can she hear my heart sing out to her? Does she know every guitar needs a stand? I'm solid, babe. I am forever. Should I tell her God sent down a defibrillator to me, my salvation and that sharing flesh is the lowest level of my love, that I can hold space her?

She drops her outfit to the ground, and I wince. It's not about the sex. I dropped my guard down to the ground too. I'll come back a thousand lifetimes if I have to—some love unions are destined on that great celestial timeline. I'll take my chance. Win or lose, I care for her. And she's so freaking hot.

On my knees I cradle her waist. I fall hard like a dying star falling deep into her earthly brown eyes as she looks down on me. I kiss her lips and she leads me to our bed. Two souls become one.

ς

Maybe it was the scent of fresh coffee brewing that woke her up. She's in my bed, she's mine. I love watching the sun rise but watching her sit up and rub the chunks of sleep from her eyes is heavenly. God, she's my love. I have the weathered box under in my hand.

She rolled over into my arms, her face on my chest. I love her so much. I hold my mother's wedding ring in my hand. I hold this woman in my other. I love them both so much, both so strong and so beautiful. Can I be so lucky? What did I do to deserve such beauty?

"Guisy. I love you."

"I love you too, John," she replies. It's a real and deep love; I've never known love until I met you."

"Guisy, will you marry me?"

I place the box into her hands.

"John, yes. I love you."

I open the box and put the thick gold band engraved with the quote, *"United in Creator's love* we *become one Spirit"* onto my love's ring finger.

Ç

I spent time with Guisy on her reservation and it broke my preconceived beliefs of who an Indigenous person is. It forced me to dig deep to discover where it comes from inside me, exploring the relationship between sensation and perception. I decided that Guisy entering into my life was not perchance but destiny.

I love the Indigenous people of the West so much. Maybe one day we will create life and I can hold a little one close to my heart and say he is mine. Maybe a dozen if the good light bulb or Creator or whatever shines His life on me; or Her.

Our marriage vows took place in the Sacred Sweat lodge of her people. There, in ceremony, we were wrapped in one blanket blessed by Great Spirit, bound together here on Earth until death. It was beautiful. I walked into the lodge sun wise with a prayer on my lips for all things and all beings. I see Guisy as a precious being as well, deserving of all my love and we together walking into the universe as one.

Chapter Fourteen

Allen Wench, Wrenching my Heart

Since when does her name become my verb?

Upon our return to Los Angeles, she was quickly scouted by a producer and whisked away to film a documentary leaving me in the dust; maybe we will film our movie together this summer? Maybe we can honeymoon when she gets back? After all, this is her dream come true.

I text my doll, but she doesn't answer. I try every app on my phone and still no response. I feel like giving up.

It's hard, you know, but I've managed to express how I feel. I learned how to communicate with her and put it to practice. Let go and wait. She's doing her own thing, and I love her for it.

But I'll go mad if I stay here waiting for her. I'll go to New York and check out the Met with some of my old crew that I haven't seen in so long. Man, I've changed. I know she's in New York, I can't wait to see her, and I'll surprise her!

Ç

New York is beautiful. The art scene is amazing too, and the food…oh my God, the food. I lose myself in thought for a while, then that's when the cover of a magazine on the table beside me catches my eye.

Guisy's picture is on the bottom corner with a page number dangling over her. She's gorgeous. I lunge over and grab it, tracing my fingers over her face. She's in town. She's at a local playhouse. *If I race there, I might make it on time. Fuck!*

Of course, time means nothing and screws me over bad. The doors are locked, and the lights are off. I missed my girl and her show.

Where the hell is she? Why won't she pick up my calls or my texts? Sad as hell, I walk and walk until exhaustion overtakes me. Defeat almost kills me. I miss her so bad. Life isn't fair. I've done so much good you think things would go right for me, right?

Just as I wave a taxi down, I peer into a fancy restaurant window and there's my girl, sitting with some stiff in a suit. Holy shit I'm pissed off, but I'm excited at the same time.

I storm into that laudy daudy foodie place and stand behind her as she lets him touch her hands and hold them over their plates. He glares at me like I'm a bum from the streets. So, I bend down, grab his glass of wine, and guzzle it down. Then, I crack my knuckles.

How could she do this to me? Gross, I hate apple juice.

When she turns her head and looks up at me, her eyes bulge like she's seen a ghost.

"Really? This is what you've being doing?" I yell at her, not even giving her a chance to speak. "Fucking around on me with this old guy? Older than me! You got something for old men, Guisy?"

I turn in a rage and walk out into the foyer pissed off beyond belief.

Unbelievable! She's just sitting yakking with her new boyfriend or old man thing. Really Guisy Rose Bobb!

I strain my eyes trying to see if they're looking all lustfully at each other.

Disgusting. More men are joining their table. Now, they're pushing their books on her? Wait.

I wish I had my glasses right now.

A lady is standing beside them. They're all holding hands. I can hear them talking to each other. But why are they holding hands?

My stomach broils with jealousy. *Where is this coming from?* Then Guisy kisses one man on the cheek, smiling, looking at him with love in her eyes.

My mind tells me to stay, but my body runs.

Chapter Fifteen

The Dying Star

I ran from her straight into the arms of whiskey, my first girl. I can't do this, it's too fucking hard. She's too good for me. I knew it from the very first day I met her. I used her ass then and, even without trying, I did it again and there's no going back.

Ç

He won't answer. I lost him. I lose everyone I love. I'll pray. I'll pray and ask Spirit for guidance and protection for my John boy. I love him. My pain was off the hook, so I gave it to Spirit.

"Lead me, Spirit. Let's go together."

Ç

Red Bull—thank God for Red Bull and Jaeger. It'll keep me up for this long drive.

Shitty part about driving thirty-seven hours with only a cat nap is that the eyes start to burn and it's hard to focus. But if I keep on driving with the windows down, music on, and chain smoke the night away, maybe, just maybe, I'll make it there just before dawn. Which, by the way, is my favorite time of the day (or is it night?). Fuck.

This night is unreal, the air so clear of smog that you can see every detail of every star above. It's spectacular because of all the falling stars. Man, I made like a dozen wishes. I can see her face so clear now. Maybe I'll call her as soon as I get to the ranch.

Yeah, ya only live once! Hey, where's my cigarette? Yeah, I'm feeling pretty good now. Hope is a bitch!

But I drifted off.

By the time I woke up…it was too late. I should have buckled. I should have called her to hear her voice.

Flight. My car flew, soared like an eagle. My head hit the windshield. My shoulder crushed up against the frame above the door. Shit. Fucking stars. I am one with them. I'm dying.

Chapter Sixteen

Let's Just Kiss!

I grew up pauper, raised by a pauper. But the mountain boy from Montana grew tired of the small-town life.

I worked in the mill long enough to buy my first bike and leather jacket. The grease that I used to polish my dad's boots I used on my own. Together, we slicked our hair back and hit up the saloon. Dad was a lush, but he provided for us the best he could, and it helped that every weekend we racked them up and made a few bucks sinking balls. Before me, it was grandfather and dad. When Ma started nagging me that it was about time to settle down and put up my own house, maybe a trailer to start off with...I started to think.

I almost settled. I almost did it. They set me up with a filly at the annual barn dance and I rebelled and got wasted. I danced with every girl there and, that night, time stood still. My chest felt like it was going to explode as I watched my family and friends like I was on the outside of a television. My heart sank. I was losing it and starting to freak out on the inside.

I didn't want a clothesline welcoming me home. No sand boxes. No swing set. And never ever did I want to take my bi-weekly paycheck to my bank, cash it, take it home, pay the bills, buy the food, fix up the house, buy kids shit, take her out to the beauty salon, and be broke the next day. No fucking way. I didn't want no bare foot, swollen belly old lady nagging on me night and day. I didn't want to grow old and worn out and so fucking full of regret that my heart was giving out by my fiftieth, like my pa and his pa.

Hell no.

So, I did what not that many do: take the narrow road. That road to freedom. I revel in rising above.

Before dawn could squander my day, I packed my shit up and jumped on my bike not knowing where life would take me. All I could do was ride. I lit my smoke and inhaled right deep as I looked back in my side mirror. That was the last time my eyes saw home. All were asleep but one. My little sister stood at the front window, in our tiny box home, glumly waving goodbye.

All this Midwest boy could think of was seeing the ocean; seen lots of movies and what always stood out was any setting swooning me, lulling my imagination of diving into rolling, continual, wild waves—like me.

So that was it. My wallet fat, no care in the world, I drove west. It was supposed to be a long and painful drive, but to me it was heaven.

I found work. The town was sizzling hot. I wasn't used to the sunshine, but I never missed the rain. My eyes were blinded though and the only way I could adjust was by wearing shades, 24/7.

I know I stood out like a fucking sore thumb. Everybody dressed the same. Weird pants all flared out at the crotch like women's bloomers, elastics at the ankles. They wore bright-colored dress shirts with padding on the shoulders.

Holy shit they looked funny; it was fucking hilarious and they looked at me like *I* was weird! Wranglers, white T-shirt, a logger's belt and my good old faithful black work boots. I wouldn't trade them in for the world. I ain't no clown. Still ain't.

When I was walking out of a so-called bar—a titty bar in fact—a red head took a picture of me with her big camera. Then she came right up to me with her hands in front of her face, floating in the air in the shape of a box. I thought she was going to hit on me when she grabbed my face, her eyes squinting. She smiled and asked me if I was looking for work. I laughed at her and asked her the same thing. I thought maybe she was one of those ladies of the night or something.

Turned out she was some movie producer's assistant or secretary or something like that. She brought me to some place called Universal. There, a sheet was given to me. I stood there not knowing what the fuck to do. I read the lines, the wrong lines I might add. She came up to me and told me to read it over again. "Picture the scene in your head," she said. "Use your imagination."

Oh, that's easy. Try working in some mill twelve hours a day. I do it all the time.

All I used to dream about was leaving that dead-end town. So, I was about to read the sentence and I figured *fuck it*. I chucked the sheet on the ground below me and shook my head. I was a man, a gangster, a hardcore kid. So, I became him, and it was smooth like butter.

I was hired on the spot. She told me to never change my look or who I was. Hollywood will love you. And she did.

Years ago, I invested a fuckload of cash into some technology business. There were no returns, ever. I forgot about it. Then I got a letter. They wanted to buy my stock back. That made me wonder why, so I googled it and found out that tech company was doing well. I was rich. Of course, I declined to sell. They sent me comp gifts all the time. I dig that shit.

Today, virtual reality is where it's at. VR video games are my thing. Then my imagination kicked in and I decided I wanted to make my own VR movies or series or something. Where to start?

Then she came into my mind.

"Babe!" I yelled. My rift and touch are still on me. I move around and get off the bed. What the fuck? Why won't she answer me? My hands motion forward to touch her. She's looking at me. Why isn't she answering me back? Am I dreaming or something? I close my eyes, thinking when I open them, all will be normal again. I just want to hold my girl and kiss her. That's all I need. I made it this far to see her. Home again.

Home? Where am I?

ς

"His eyes are open. Is he awake?" I look in the mirror behind John's bed. My brows sit like two crowns of thorns above my chocolate-brown, sorrowful eyes.

"No, he is not." The stern doctor is honest with me, making sure there is no emotion in his voice, no notes of hope.

"Is he dead?"

"He has suffered and sustained major brain injuries. His results however indicate he has a rare condition called AVM, Arteriovenous Malformation. An AVM is a tangle of abnormal and poorly formed blood vessels. They have a higher rate of bleeding than normal vessels. AVMs can occur anywhere in the body," the doc says, but it's mostly over my head. He continues, "Brain AVMs are of special concern because of the damage they cause when they bleed. They are very rare and occur in less than 1% of the general population. John is in the 1%."

"Can he hear us?" I whisper.

"That is not clear." Slightly annoyed, he talks to me with his back turned, signing off on John's medical file.

Don't mess with a Native lady.

"Let me make this clear. He can hear me. Now I want *you* to hear me. Fix it now! I know enough that if we waste time fucking around, he will never come back to me. Fix it now. Surgery now. Money is no problem. If you can't do it, I will find the best. I want him fixed now or God help you!"

Ç

No. Oh God, no!

I hear a pop between my ears. I smell something burning. Everything is getting dim. I'm getting cold. No…

I start to cry. I'm stuck in God's 3D Toy box.

Chapter Seventeen

Alan Smithee

"I will let you down,

I will make you hurt.

I'll wear this crown of thorns."

—*Nine Inch Nails*

The metal roof made the falling rain bounce, tapping and knocking in the most organic paradiddle, calling out to the broken, "Awake!" It spun on repeat for days until its job was done, yet John remained motionless.

During the day, the hallway was noisy and full of hospital staff and orderlies. During the evening, they closed all doors and dimmed the lights. The only movement was the housekeep running the electric floor cleaner up and down the hallway. The machine hummed in time with the flat notes buzzing from the long fluorescent light bulbs.

This eve though, I noticed his blinds were forgotten and left open, until a young housekeeper entered the room to empty the garbage bin and restock my bathroom items. She noticed the blinds and drew them close. They hit the windowsill with a *thud*, making my eyes squint and glare. The young employee bowed her head down and quickly left the room.

Then I saw it. I grew excited with hope. I noticed his stirring. Maybe it was the rain. Maybe it was the staff. I don't care what woke him up. Then his body flinched, and his chest soared higher and higher filling itself with determination. *Good old John…what a fighter!* I rose to my feet.

His hands moved from his sides up to his face pulling on the tubes that were connected to a drip of saline solution and nutrients. He flinched from the pain, either sore from the accident, the intensive surgery, or the needles connected to his veins.

His hands darted over his eyes like a baby searching its mother for its first feed. Shock and realization, maybe fear, etched his eyebrows and pursed his dry lips. What was he looking for? He was confused. I was elated.

ς

Slowly, I open my eyes, lids drawing over my pupils. It feels like sandpaper scraping. The pain is immeasurable. When my lids bat up and down, I try to focus, searching for light, any light to tell me where I am.

I want to call out a name, but my mind goes blank. I bolt up and start to shake, my eyes watering in pain or anguish or grief, I'm not sure.

Someone calls for the doctor and a flurry of nurses and medical staff usher to my side. A clear, small bag of liquid is quickly fed into my tubes, making my shoulders relax, and I fall back into my metal bed covered with stiff, starched sheets. I see a hand holding the metal side rail. I look up into a face radiating joy, calling out my name.

"John. It's me. My love, you're alive," she says.

The nurse brings a paper cup filled with cubes and water to my lips after raising the bed up into a sitting position. I'm ravenous. I take my fill and thank her, the water replenishing my zeal and zest. I open my eyes again.

She has a wet cloth in her hands, smiling a beautiful grin. She dabs it over my eyes, my mouth, and my chin then slowly smooths it over my forehead. There she plants a sweet, enduring kiss. Tears flow down my cheeks, tickling my ears.

The doctor orders her out of the room for examination. She smiles at me and stands outside my hospital room door then waves at me before I'm lowered down for tests.

"Ma'am, you can come back in now." The kind doctor closes the metal file and clips it on my footboard as she reenters the room." John, you've being in a vehicle accident and have suffered extensive injuries. Your wife agreed to stay, and we corrected all damage through surgery. You're lucky to be alive."

"Oh? Thank you. I don't remember anything," I reply in shock as I look over the doctor, my wife and then finally my thin body.

"Hunny, you've being in recovery for three weeks. You should be ready to go home by the weekend. I'm so glad you're alive." The pretty woman holds my hand, kissing each finger. She closes her eyes and starts to pray. Being in her presence, I also bow my head and listen to her sweet voice. Maybe there is a God? Maybe that's why I'm alive. My wife is beautiful.

But who is she?

"Sorry. This is a dumb question, but what's your name?" My big eyes glisten with hope and embarrassment.

"Your memory will be foggy and short, but we will rebuild, hunny. Make all new memories; you and me. My name is Guisy."

The doctor pats my back and smiles. "John, she hasn't left your side. She willed you back to life. You weren't responding, your will was broken. She stood over you and prayed for you night and day, fasting and giving it all up to the Lord, Creator, for you. You've got a good woman."

Guisy hugs the doctor before he leaves the small hospital room. Then she takes my blanket off and puts a new clean one over my legs. She's still sniffling from crying, melting my heart. My hands respond by holding her as tight as I could until I drift off, back into sleep.

Chapter Eighteen

Tail Piece

Together we dusted off mom's kitchen table and hutch that was passed down throughout the generations. Dad's chair in the front room was well built. I felt odd, almost damn naughty sitting in his spot. Tiny memories usurped me at a slow and steady pace.

Guisy found work right fast as we were short on cash and I was still a mess. My hospital bills and everything else wiped us out financially. My face, she told me, was once perfect. Now, it's mangled and scarred, my jaw shifted slightly to the right. One eye lid will always be lazy, and my memory was short. The scar tissue on my scalp was itchy and tender. I looked like Frankenstein, but she still loved me. She still wanted me.

There were long gaps of time where all I could do was sit or lie down. I had no sharp comebacks, no more snarky remarks. Doc said the gaps of nothingness were my mind's way of self-healing.

Her patience could move the mountains; her love encompassing above measure. She didn't seem to mind me clinging to some manliness and delving into football—the Grizzlies rocked it. She cooked. She cleaned the bathroom and the kitchen, brought the garbage out and even bucked up a cord of wood to fuel our fire.

Fire...there was none in our bedroom. I slept on our couch; I had no desire. She was gorgeous to look at, but nothing could move me to take her by my side.

The brain injury support group helped me a bit. She didn't want me to go. She said her love was enough. She said she gave up her past life for us. Deep down, I felt I owed her something, part of me. But parts of me were already missing, maybe from the accident, I think. I don't think I'll ever gain my past back. According to her, I shouldn't want it. It wasn't good for me, or her.

I owed her something, after all. She worked her ass off in town with two part-time jobs. So, I decided to ask for help. My counselor from group therapy helped me put together a resume and he even drove me all over town, practically holding my hand as we went from this store to that.

I started to get stressed. Not one call for an interview, not one bite. No one wanted to hire a wreck of a man. No one would give me a chance. Not even the mill my dad and *his* dad worked at. I was thinking maybe they could honor my family, something like that.

I knew Christmas was coming and bills were mounting. With time, the debts would snowball and roll down that hill of life and squish me. I could feel pain radiating throughout my chest kicking my lungs out, making it hard to breathe. Anxiety is a bitch. Brain damage is a fucking thorn.

Worse though...something was missing. Something felt just not right, and I couldn't shake it no matter how hard I tried.

Guisy aged quickly. My babe's mane wasn't kept up. She gained major weight and started to frump right out. I felt bad for her, but I didn't feel compelled to nag her. I just bided time and started to walk for exercise and meditate to relieve some stress.

The Native reservation was a mile out of town. Eventually I gained enough endurance, one day at a time, to move forward. I journeyed, sojourned into their beautiful valley between two hills. Of course, I was nervous—never been on no Injun village before—but something drew me in. I became lost in her hills.

Their roads were paved, sidewalks fragranced by the apple orchards and the rows upon rows of Bing cherries: Life.

The first building I came across looked like a busy place. The sign above the door read "Health Administration" and an all-familiar scent hit me: fried bread—bannock—the bread of love. *What the fuck? Where did that come from?* The receptionist was smiling and offered to tour me throughout the building without me even asking. Maybe my spirit said it all.

She led me to an office and asked me to fill out paperwork. One sheet was a criminal record check. I obliged, just honored to be close to something yummy. I knew we were close because I heard the clanging of dishes in a nearby kitchen. She left me to finish the employment application and, when I was done, I ventured quickly to somewhere familiar. *Maybe I have been here before?*

I walked through the doors and was surprised by the setup. It was a recreation center. There were old people, young couples, kids and babies sitting all over at round tables. Murals of eagles, buffalo, salmon and the four directions beckoned me home. I walked until I hit the kitchen. There, ready to serve me, was an elderly native woman full of smiles with warm, brown, chocolate eyes.

The following day, I started work as the resident repairman, security, and backup cook. And I loved every day of my job. At times, I couldn't believe I was taking their money. They thought I was helping them. But it was these people, these lovely souls nurturing me, that moved me forward.

One of the volunteers didn't show up, so Auntie asked me to either cook up the lunch or read to the children. I love kids. I think I always wanted one, or a dozen, so I quickly cleaned myself up and set up rows of tiny little wooden chairs. I wiped each one down and put a little snack beneath each: a bag of chips, a water bottle, and a peanut-free granola bar that I picked up in town as a treat for the wee ones. It made me happy to give back to my community.

Slowly, parents trickled in and they all sat close to the open kitchen sipping their coffee and colas, nibbling on veggies and fruit.

I sat and waited, animated and ready to connect. Book in hand, I cleared my throat and started in character. I took them away to another land, theatrically trained, and we flourished.

Theatrically trained? Yes, I think I am. I was, I mean.

Minutes later, a Child Protection Agent came up to me and interrupted the story. A small child was standing behind her. The agent pulled up an adult chair and pointed for the child to sit. Then she left.

I enunciated slowly and as kind as I could to engage the child. But her shoulders slumped. Her long, black, messy hair covered her chest and all her face. Her little white Keds, well-used and not so white, hung loosely on her tiny feet far above the ground like meat hooks. She was pitiful.

The children beside her scrunched their noses and held them tight, reacting in a delicate way as not to chastise their comrade of war. My heart was falling to an all-familiar place of unknown. Broken, my heart; and Auntie's too. You can't mess with an elder woman who loves her people so fucking much she'd kill for them, die for them.

Auntie pulled a chair up beside Broken and sat quietly, listening to our story. Her gnarled hand slowly moved to the child's. The children quit making their funny noises and their youthful chirps. Auntie pulled a sweater out from her bingo bag. She warmed the hand, relaxing the broken one. Her ancient momma hand lightly touched a shoulder then moved her long crown over to her back. The wee one tilted her head and looked down at Auntie's white nurse shoes. She slipped the handknitted purple sweater onto the child. Broken smiled at Auntie and quickly moved up onto her lap.

It was then, when she held her dimpled chin up, that I cried. Soundless and moved, I witnessed the calm and comfort on her tiny little face as the elder smoothed her hair down into place and tenderly gave her love and affection. The little child looked up at me. She was the sweetest thing I've ever seen in my life. Her eyes were worn and had seen much devastation.

I see you there, little one.

I feel a small crack in my concrete walls, holding my memory of her back.

This wee girl reminds me of someone.

I've searched for her repeatedly. No Face.

And here she is, coming to me, resuscitating and giving me life: Little doctor.

That face, those brown eyes. She reminds me of a place I once was. A reservation I once fell in love with. Children I helped save. Of a native woman who once saved me.

Walls shatter, and there in my memory was her: Jay.

God!

ς

It felt like such a long drive back to her.

I reflected as memory came to me, like pouring thick cream into a black coffee. And I reveled in it. All I want is her.

I raced through the door only to find an empty house. A note sat on our kitchen table. It read, "I've gone home. I can't do this anymore."

ς

After several weeks trying to convince my family doctor to grant me permission to travel, I celebrated! I had medication that would help my brain cope with elevation and hopefully I could make it across the States without a brain bleed.

I remembered our wedding ceremony in our Sacred Sweat Lodge, and so I called upon Creator to join me on this journey.

I would never let her go. She's my medicine. I want to spend the rest of my days with my babe.

I packed my bag. I knew it would be a long drive back to Seattle, to the reserve she came from. I slept a lot these days, so I'd have to pull over many times to be safe.

Ç

When I finally got to Guisy's band office, the Chief greets me as if I was family—our embrace is long and much needed.

"Where is Guisy?" I ask the aged man donning his cowboy hat.

He walks me outside, to the back field. Then he points. "There, she's there."

I want to die. He points to a grave site, a graveyard. His head lowers. A sharp pain shoots through my chest finding space in my shoulders.

God, no. No! I scream but nothing comes out of my voice box except a loud, tight sigh. My tear ducts damaged from my accident, I cry on the inside. Fucking God! What have you done?

The graveyard is gloomy but for a few bushels of flowers. Each cross is pauper with no names, no headstones. I don't know which one is hers. The Chief leaves me.

I walk to the freshest mound of dirt and fall to my knees. I decide I want to die.

Now that I remember her, life without her is no life at all. How and why would God take her? *Take me for fuck's sake!* The good always die young.

I shake so hard my whole body reacts in shock. I can barely breathe.

"Hey mister, it's getting dark. Not supposed to be in our graveyard when it's dark. It's against the rules, dontcha know?" someone calls out. "Didn't your mama teach you that?"

"Leave me," I cry. My swollen eyes don't want to look upon anyone ever again.

"Hey! I just cleaned up that grave. Watch out. I have to nail this plaque up." I get up off my knees, and she shoves me gently before hammering away. I drop back down to my knees then she kneels beside me.

"Come on. I have to lock the gate up. Want a cup of java?" she chirps. Bloody hell, what a rude little woman.

I get up and start to follow her until she stops and turns to me. Her baseball hat barely covers her messy hair flowing all over her small, courteous shoulders. I stop walking, mad at her mostly because I'm pissed and hurt and need a bottle of whiskey. I turn towards her ready to rage. Then I pause. She takes off her baseball cap and I pull out my glasses and put them on as fast as I can.

"Johnny boy, my love, is that you?"

I fall to my knees in silence, crying.

CPSIA information can be obtained
at www.ICGtesting.com
Printed in the USA
LVHW032129010821
694269LV00007B/1394

9 781999 496128